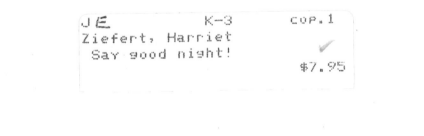

HELLO READING!

"HELLO READING™ books are a perfect introduction to reading. Brief sentences full of word repetition and full-color pictures stress visual clues to help a child take the first important steps toward reading. Mastering HELLO READING™ books will build children's reading confidence and give them the enthusiasm to stand on their own in the world of words."

—Bee Cullinan
Past President of the International Reading
Association, Professor in New York University's
Early Childhood and Elementary Education Program

"Readers aren't born, they're made. Desire is planted—planted by parents who work at it."

—Jim Trelease
author of *The Read Aloud Handbook*

"When I was a classroom reading teacher, I recognized the importance of good stories in making children understand that reading is more than just recognizing words. I saw that children who get excited about reading and who have ready access to books make noticeably greater gains in reading comprehension and fluency. The development of the HELLO READING™ series grows out of this experience."

—Harriet Ziefert
M.A.T., New York University School of Education
Author, Language Arts Module,
Scholastic Early Childhood Program

For A.M.B., who knows
good dreams come on good nights

VIKING KESTREL
Viking Penguin Inc., 40 West 23rd Street,
New York, New York 10010, U.S.A.
Penguin Books Ltd., Harmondsworth, Middlesex, England
Penguin Books Australia Ltd., Ringwood, Victoria, Australia
Penguin Books Canada Limited, 2801 John St., Markham, Ontario, Canada
Penguin Books (N.Z.) Ltd., 182–190 Wairau Rd., Auckland 10, New Zealand

First published in 1987
Published simultaneously in Canada
Text copyright © Harriet Ziefert, 1987
Illustrations copyright © Catherine Siracusa, 1987
All rights reserved

ISBN 0-670-81722-8 Library of Congress Catalog Card No: 86-40478
Printed in Singapore for Harriet Ziefert, Inc.
HELLO READING is a trademark of Harriet Ziefert, Inc.

Say Good Night!

Harriet Ziefert
Illustrated by Catherine Siracusa

JE
cop. 1

VIKING KESTREL

Now say good night,
they say.
Now say good night.

But I don't want
to say good night.

Why *good?* I ask.
What's good
about the night?

Tell me.

On a good night
you can see the moon.

And moons are nice.

On a good night
you can hear quiet.

And quiet is nice.

Warm breezes come
on good nights.

And breezes are nice.

Good dreams come
on good nights.
And dreams are nice.

So say
good night.
Good night
good night
good …

night!

All right, good night!
Turn off my light.

Sleep tight
Sleep tight
Till morning light.

Now say good morning,
they say.
Now say good morning.

Why *good?* I ask.
What's good
about the morning?

On a good morning
you can see the sun.

You can smell
bacon and eggs

and hear music
from the radio.

So say
good morning.

Good morning good
morning good…

morning!

All right, good morning!

cop.1

I'm up!